TALES FROM BEYOND

Deadly Fortune | The Attic | Unbreakable

WRITTEN, DIRECTED, AND PRODUCED BY Kevin Herren and Jim O'Rear.
STARRING: Kyle Hebert, Mary Elizabeth McGlynn, Jim O'Rear, Robert Picardo, Daniel Roebuck, and Betsy Rue

Schiffer Publishing Ltd

4880 Lower Valley Road • Atglen, PA 19310

Written, directed, and produced by Kevin Herren and Jim O'Rear.
Recorded in part at In Fidelity Recordings, Los Angeles, California.
Special Thanks to Paula Clark, Mark Lawrence, Victor Rivera, and Corey Drick.
Original score written and performed by Virgil Franklin.

Cover image: Midnight Treetops In Fog © MrEco99. www.bigstockphoto.com

Title Page image: The cast of Tales From Beyond: Jim O'Rear, Kyle Hebert, Betsy Rue, Robert Picardo, Mary Elizabeth McGlynn, and Daniel Roebuck.

Copyright © 2014 by Kevin Herren and Jim O'Rear

Library of Congress Control Number: 2014944669

All rights reserved. No part of this work may be reproduced or used in any form or by any means—graphic, electronic, or mechanical, including photocopying or information storage and retrieval systems—without written permission from the publisher.

The scanning, uploading and distribution of this book or any part thereof via the Internet or via any other means without the permission of the publisher is illegal and punishable by law. Please purchase only authorized editions and do not participate in or encourage the electronic piracy of copyrighted materials.

"Schiffer," "Schiffer Publishing, Ltd. & Design," and the "Design of pen and inkwell" are registered trademarks of Schiffer Publishing, Ltd.

Type set in Trajan Pro/Univers LT Std/Minion Pro
ISBN: 978-0-7643-4762-7
Printed in China

Published by Schiffer Publishing, Ltd.
4880 Lower Valley Road
Atglen, PA 19310
Phone: (610) 593-1777; Fax: (610) 593-2002
E-mail: Info@schifferbooks.com

For the largest selection of fine reference books on this and related subjects, please visit our website at www.schifferbooks.com.
You may also write for a free catalog.

This book may be purchased from the publisher.
Please try your bookstore first.

We are always looking for people to write books on new and related subjects.
If you have an idea for a book, please contact us at proposals@schifferbooks.com

Schiffer Books are available at special discounts for bulk purchases for sales promotions or premiums. Special editions, including personalized covers, corporate imprints, and excerpts can be created in large quantities for special needs. For more information contact the publisher.

Contents

Introduction
4

Deadly Fortune
5

The Attic
21

Unbreakable
35

Photo Gallery
49

INTRODUCTION

Daniel Roebuck. (*Lost, Matlock, The Fugitive, Glee, The Devil's Rejects, Halloween 2.*)

Radio drama (or audio drama, audio play, radio play, radio theater) is a dramatized, purely acoustic performance, broadcast on radio or published on audio media, such as tape or CD. With no visual component, radio drama depends on dialogue, music, and sound effects to help the listener imagine the characters and story.

Radio drama traces its roots back to the 1880s in France. English-language radio drama seems to have started in the United States in the 1920s. A "Rural Line on Education," a brief sketch specifically written for radio, aired on Pittsburgh's KDKA in 1921. Newspaper accounts of the era report on a number of other drama experiments by America's commercial radio stations: KYW broadcast a season of complete operas from Chicago starting in November 1921. In February 1922, entire Broadway musical comedies with the original casts aired from WJZ's Newark studios. Actors Grace George and Herbert Hayes performed an entire play from a San Francisco station in the summer of 1922.

Radio drama achieved widespread popularity within a decade of its initial development in the 1920s. By the 1940s, it was considered a leader in popular entertainment internationally. With the advent of television in the 1950s, however, radio drama lost some of its popularity, and in some countries has never regained large audiences. However, recordings of "old-time radio" survive today in the audio archives of collectors and museums, as well as several online sites such as Internet Archive.

Today, radio drama has a minimal presence on terrestrial radio in the United States. Much of American radio drama is restricted to rebroadcasts or podcasts of programs from previous decades. However, other nations still have thriving traditions of radio drama. In the United Kingdom, for example, the BBC produces and broadcasts hundreds of new radio plays each year on Radio 3, Radio 4, and Radio 4 Extra. Podcasting has also offered the means of creating new radio dramas, in addition to the distribution of vintage programs.

Jim O'Rear and Kevin Herren have produced *Tales From Beyond* and other audio productions with the hopes of introducing this lost art to a new generation and to rekindle the popularity of this unique art form.

DEADLY FORTUNE

CAST OF CHARACTERS (in order of appearance)

Narrator:	Daniel Roebuck
Game Barker:	Jim O'Rear
Jane:	Betsy Rue
Bob:	Robert Picardo
Madam Lavanya:	Mary Elizabeth McGlynn
Cab Driver:	Daniel Roebuck
Conductor:	Kyle Hebert
Porter:	Kyle Hebert
Lady:	Mary Elizabeth McGlynn
Waiter:	Kyle Hebert

Serious work ensues as Robert Picardo, Betsy Rue, and Mary Elizabeth McGlynn record scenes for "Deadly Fortune."

[MUSIC IN AND UNDER]

NARRATOR: Don't you just love a carnival? The crisp fall air; the smell of corn dogs and funnel cakes; music, games, side shows and…gypsy fortune tellers. Join me for our next tale as we follow a couple as they enjoy all the sights and sounds of a fall carnival…in a story we call…"Deadly Fortune."

GAME BARKER: Step right up, three balls for five dollars. Knock down all the pins; win a prize, win a prize. You…young man! Come win that girl of yours a prize.

JANE: Come on, Bobby, let's go get some food. You know all these games are rigged.

BOB: No…No…I got this. I used to play baseball in school. This'll be easy. No problem.

GAME BARKER: Come on…step right up and win that lady a prize. Five dollars gets you three throws.

BOB: All right, here ya go; five dollars. Better step back old man; don't want you to get hurt with my fastball!

GAME BARKER: HA! Whatever you say son…whatEVER you say. [chuckling]

SOUND: [BALL HITTING BACKSTOP]

GAME BARKER: Ohhhhh, too bad, too bad. Try again, son; two throws left.

JANE: Come on, Bobby! You can do it!

SOUND: [BALL HITTING BACKSTOP]

GAME BARKER: Son that "fast ball" of yours sure looks like a curve ball to me. [laughing] One more throw! Better make this one count.

SOUND: [BALL HITTING BACKSTOP]

GAME BARKER: Oh, too bad. Here you go, try again. Three balls for five dollars.

BOB: Yeah, right! I don't think so! Come on Jane, let's go. I told you it's rigged. Let's get some funnel cake.

JANE: [confused] Yeah…yeah…sure thing.

GAME BARKER: Step right up, three balls for five dollars. Knock down all the pins; win a prize.

SOUND: [FOOTSTEPS WALKING]

JANE: Oh, Bobby…Look! It's a fortune teller!

BOB: You don't really believe that stuff…do you?

JANE: No….not really, but let's do it anyway. It'll be fun. Pleeeeease?

BOB: [frustrated] Fine…whatever.

[MUSIC FADES OUT]

MADAM LAVANYA: Welcome…come in, come in. I'm Madam Lavanya. Sit…sit.

JANE: Come on Bobby. You do it. Let her read your fortune.

BOB: No way! All these crazy fortune tellers are frauds. It's not REAL.

MADAM LAVANYA: Please…sit. I see stormy times ahead for you both.

SOUND: [THUNDER DISTANT]

BOB: Yeah, right! HA! Even I can tell you there's a storm coming. I can HEAR…THE…THUNDER. [laughing]

JANE: Oh, come on, Bobby. Play along. For me? Pleeeease?

BOB: Fine….Whatever. Hey, where's your crystal ball?

MADAM LAVANYA: No crystal ball. Take my hand and be silent. I have to concentrate. [deep, heavy breath] I see a train. Many… many trains.

BOB: Now, Jane…you know I'm flying back to Chicago tonight. Trains? See…this is CRAZY.

MADAM LAVANYA: SILENCE! [deep, heavy breath] Many trains…and people. Many people. So much noise. Confusion and noise. Fifty-nine.

BOB: Fifty-nine what? Bottles of beer on the wall? [laughing]

JANE: Oh, Bobby, be quiet…listen.

MADAM LAVANYA: The train…Fifty-nine…Car fifty-nine. So much confusion…So much noise…an umbrella…not his.

BOB: This is crazy. She's not even making sense.

JANE: SHHHH. Listen to her, Bobby.

MADAM LAVANYA: An umbrella…not his…Dee…I see the letter D.

BOB: Yeah, for DUMB.

MADAM LAVANYA: Fifty-nine D…compartment D…train…

BOB: Listen…I'm flying back to Chicago on a PLANE…you know…in the AIR.

JANE: Bobby, I don't think she can hear you anymore. Be quiet. Listen.

MADAM LAVANYA: Bright blue dress. Beau-ti-ful. A bird…a shining silver locket. For a love that endures all time.

JANE: Awwwww, how romantic.

MADAM LAVANYA: He's nervous. He spills her drink! So nervous.

JANE: Hey! Who is this woman and why are you spilling her drink?

BOB: SHHH… [sarcastically] Be quiet, Jane. Listen to her.

MADAM LAVANYA: He is scared. Running! Running! So scared!

BOB: Yeah, right! Sure I am.

MADAM LAVANYA: Running! She has a knife! A knife! Running! Falling! She's standing over him with a knife! Nooooooooooo!!!

SOUND: [THUNDER]

JANE: What does it mean?

BOB: It doesn't mean anything. Crazy ramblings from an old, crazy woman.

MADAM LAVANYA: [nervous] You….You go now.

BOB: Yeah, whatever. What do we owe you?

MADAM LAVANYA: [more nervous] Nothing…Nothing…Just go.

SOUND: [THUNDER]

JANE: Maybe we should go, Bobby. Sounds like the storm is getting closer.

BOB: Come on. I'll take you home. I've got to get to the airport anyway.

[MUSIC SCENE TRANSITION]

NARRATOR: Back at Jane's apartment, the sounds of the approaching storm echo in the distance.

JANE: Do you have to go?

BOB: You know I do. I've got that big meeting on Monday and I still have to prepare for it.

SOUND: [THUNDER]

JANE: But, I'm worried. The storm...and what the gypsy said.

BOB: She's just a senile old woman. Don't worry. It's just a bunch of mumbo jumbo anyway. I've got to go or I'll miss my flight.

JANE: Okay, but call me the minute your plane lands.

BOB: I will. The minute I'm back in Chicago.

[MUSIC SCENE TRANSITION]

NARRATOR: Later that night, as the storm rages on, there's a knock at Jane's door.

SOUND: [DOOR KNOCK, THUNDER]

JANE: [quietly to herself] Now, who could that be? [out loud] Coming! Who is it?

BOB: It's me, Jane. Open up!

SOUND: [DOOR UNLOCK, OPEN, THUNDER, RAIN, WIND]

JANE: Bob, what are you doing back here? You'll miss your flight! Come in out of the rain!

SOUND: [DOOR CLOSE, THUNDER]

BOB: Well, funny thing. With this storm, traffic was horrible. And I DID miss my flight. Seems there aren't any more flights leaving tonight from New York to Chicago. Looks like that crazy old gypsy was right. I'm taking the train after all.

SOUND: [THUNDER]

JANE: Oh, no! Not the train!

BOB: Now, Jane, just stop it. Stop thinking about that crazy old woman. My train doesn't leave for a few hours so let's not spend it worrying about that crazy nonsense.

SOUND: [THUNDER, RAIN, STORM]

NARRATOR: But Jane did worry. With every passing minute she worried. Every clap of thunder reminded her of the fortune teller's words. The raging storm subsided just in time for Bob to leave for the train station.

SOUND: [DOOR OPENS]

JANE: Oh, Bobby, I wish you wouldn't go back tonight.

BOB: Now, Jane.

JANE: But…

BOB: But nothing! My reservation is nowhere near car fifty-nine. Look, my cab is here and I've got to go! I will call you the minute I'm back in Chicago. And don't worry. Everything will be fine.

JANE: I hope so, Bobby. Goodnight.

SOUND: [DOOR CLOSES, LOCKS]

[MUSIC SCENE TRANSITION]

SOUND: [TRAFFIC NOISE]

BOB: What the…? Driver…driver…what's going on up there?

CAB DRIVER: The weather. Everybody missed their flights and they're trying to take the train.

BOB: Just let me out here. I'll walk the rest of the way.

SOUND: [CAR DOOR OPENS AND CLOSES]

BOB: Here you go; will that cover it?

CAB DRIVER: You bet it will! And then some! Thanks! Oh…Hey, mister…wait! You forgot your umbrella!

BOB: What? Oh…no, that's not mine.

{Remembers the gyspy saying: "An umbrella…not his."}

Hmmm… [laughing] Ah, that's just a crazy coincidence.

CAB DRIVER: What?

BOB: Oh, nothing. Just thinking about something. Thanks!

SOUND: [FOOTSTEPS, CROWD NOISE]

CONDUCTOR: Yes, sir. Name, please.

BOB: Bob…Bob Kitchens.

CONDUCTOR: Let's see…

SOUND: [PAPER/PAGES TURNING]

CONDUCTOR: Here we are. Robert Kitchens. Looks like we have you in compartment A, car 22.

BOB: That's me.

CONDUCTOR: The porter will show you to your compartment.

SOUND: [FOOTSTEPS]

PORTER: Here we are, sir, twenty-two A.

SOUND: [COMPARTMENT DOOR OPENS]

BOB: Thank you.

PORTER: Yes, sir.

SOUND: [COMPARTMENT DOOR CLOSES]

BOB: [to himself] Now, for a little peace and quiet.

SOUND: [COMPARTMENT BUZZER]

BOB: [to himself] Oh, what now? [out loud] Yes, come in!

CONDUCTOR: My apologies, Mr. Kitchens. With all the confusion tonight, there seems to have been a mix-up.

BOB: Mix-up? What kind of mix-up?

CONDUCTOR: Well, you see, this lady…

BOB: Evening, ma'am.

LADY: Good evening, sir.

CONDUCTOR: Um, yes. Well…Like I was saying, this lady belongs in here. She reserved this compartment a few days ago. I'm afraid we're going to have to move you to compartment fifty-nine.

BOB: {Remembers the gypsy saying: "The train…Fifty-nine…Car fifty-nine"}

[frustrated] Wait, I don't understand. Why don't you just put the lady in the other compartment?

CONDUCTOR: Like I said, sir, the lady specifically reserved this particular space. So…

BOB: I don't care if the lady reserved the space. You put me in THIS compartment. I'm comfortable and settled and I'm NOT moving.

LADY: Oh, it's all right. I can take the other compartment.

CONDUCTOR: No…No, ma'am, it's not all right. [firmly] Now, Mr. Kitchens, as the conductor of this train, I'm responsible for the passengers. The lady reserved this space days ago and I will not have her be inconvenienced due to an error on our part. So, I'm afraid I must insist.

BOB: [irate] Well, I'm not going to be inconvenienced, either. Put the lady in the other compartment!

CONDUCTOR: Mr. Kitchens, the way I see it…you have two choices. You can either move to car fifty-nine or you can stay here in New York. The choice is yours, but you ARE NOT staying in this compartment.

BOB: Look, I've got to get back home to Chicago. But…

CONDUCTOR: Then kindly follow the porter and he will show you to your compartment. Porter, take Mr. Kitchens to fifty-nine D, please.

PORTER: Yes, sir. This way, sir.

BOB: [growling] Fine!

CONDUCTER: I'm sorry for all the confusion and inconvenience, ma'am.

LADY: It's quite all right.

SOUND: [COMPARTMENT DOOR CLOSES]

CONDUCTOR: ALL ABOARD!

SOUND: [TRAIN WHISTLE, TRAIN STARTS MOVING UP TO SPEED AND REMAINS MOVING]

SOUND: [COMPARTMENT BUZZER]

LADY: Yes?

SOUND: [COMPARTMENT DOOR OPENS]

BOB: Excuse me. I believe I left my coat.

LADY: Oh…yes, here it is.

BOB: Listen, I'm sorry about all of that before.

LADY: Oh, it's no bother.

BOB: Well, you see…I feel really bad about the whole thing and…

LADY: Yes?

BOB: Well, um…can I maybe buy you a drink in the club car?

LADY: Oh, I don't know.

BOB: Please…I really feel bad and I'd like to make it up to you.

LADY: Oh, I guess it would be all right. Let me freshen up a bit. Meet you there in a few minutes?

BOB: Sure. Looking forward to it.

SOUND: [COMPARTMENT DOOR CLOSES]

[MUSIC SCENE TRANSITION]

WAITER: Take your order, sir?

BOB: I'm waiting for someone.

WAITER: I'll check back in a few minutes, sir.

BOB: Oh, wait! Here she is.

WAITER: What'll you have miss?

LADY: Bourbon…neat.

WAITER: And for you, sir?

BOB: I'll have the same.

LADY: Sorry I took so long. I decided to change into something a little more presentable.

BOB: {Remembers the gypsy saying: "Bright blue dress. Beau-ti-ful."}

[nervous and stumbling] That's a…um…nice bright blue…um…dress.

LADY: Well, thank you—I think… [laughing] You seem nervous. Is something wrong?

BOB: Oh, no. It's just…Oh, it's nothing. Here's our drinks.

WAITER: Will there be anything else?

BOB: [impatient] No, that's all. That's…that's…thank you!

LADY: Are you sure you're okay?

BOB: Yes, yes…I'm fine. That's an interesting locket you're wearing. What is that on the front?

LADY: It's a bird of some sort. I'm not really sure. It belonged to my grandmother. My grandfather gave it to her for their fiftieth wedding anniversary. Look, he had this inscription put inside. "For a love that endures all time." Isn't that just precious?

BOB: {Remembers the gypsy saying: "A bird…a shining silver locket. For a love that endures all time"}

[very nervous] Um…that's…um…
what were you saying?

LADY: I said, isn't that precious? The inscription. "For a love that endures all time." Mr. Kitchens, are you sure you're all right?

[MUSIC IN AND UNDER]

BOB: [terrified] No…no, no, no…I'm not all right. I'm…I'm…I'm…not…not at all!

SOUND: [STUMBLING, DRINKS BEING TURNED OVER]

BOB: {Remembers the gypsy saying: "He spills her drink!"}

I'm sorry. I'm…I'm…

SOUND: [RUNNING]

LADY: Where are you going? Mr. Kitchens? Wait!

SOUND: [RUNNING]

BOB: [panting heavy breathing] Stay away!

LADY: Mr. Kitchens! Wait! What's wrong?

BOB: [out of breath] Stay away from me! Just stay away…

NARRATOR: With that last word, Bob stumbled. Trying to catch himself, he accidentally grabbed the emergency brake overhead, bringing the train to an abrupt stop.

SOUND: [SCREECHING]

[MUSIC UP AND OUT]

LADY: Welcome back, sleepy head. Just lie still, Mr. Kitchens. You're going to be all right. You had a pretty nasty cut on your head.

BOB: [groggy and confused] What? What's going on?

{Remembering the gypsy saying: "She has a knife! A knife!"}

Stay away! Don't come near me with that knife!

LADY: Now calm down. This is only a scalpel. There's nothing to be afraid of. You're lucky!

BOB: [still groggy/confused] Lucky? What…what do you mean?

LADY: Yes! Lucky I was there when you fell. Lucky I'm a doctor. But how on earth did you know?

BOB: Know? Know what?

LADY: Know to pull the emergency brake. How could you know about the other train that was stalled up ahead? How did you know? Even the engineer didn't know because the communications system was out. Who knows how many people would be dead if you hadn't pulled that emergency brake. HOW did you know?

NARRATOR: How, indeed? The gypsy fortune teller, Madame Lavanya, knew. Some may call it an incredible coincidence. Clairvoyance? Precognition? We like to call it another one of our…TALES FROM BEYOND.

THE ATTIC

CAST OF CHARACTERS (in order of appearance)

Narrator: Daniel Roebuck
Aunt Rose: Mary Elizabeth McGlynn
Ivan: Kyle Hebert
James: Robert Picardo
Mary: Betsy Rue
Alice: Mary Elizabeth McGlynn
Gas man: Jim O'Rear

Kyle Hebert uses one of his many character voices to record lines as Ivan in "The Attic."

[MUSIC IN AND UNDER]

NARRATOR: Have you ever had one of those strange experiences that you simply couldn't explain? Something so bizarre that it just doesn't make any sense to the rational mind? Something that makes you feel a little foolish when you try to tell someone about it? Well, if so, you're not alone, as you'll soon hear in another one of our TALES FROM BEYOND called "The Attic"…

AUNT ROSE: They'll be here any time now. Are their rooms ready?

IVAN: Yes, everything is ready.

AUNT ROSE: I just hope it wasn't a mistake letting them come here.

IVAN: Everything will be fine. It's good for the house to be lived in again. Good that it will have a young person here again.

AUNT ROSE: Ivan, about that young person—about Mary. You know what she's been through—the recent shock she's experienced?

IVAN: The girl's mother. Yes, terrible accident.

AUNT ROSE: We'll have to help her forget. Help occupy her time, so she's not constantly thinking about it. Oh, I don't mean she should forget her mother but…

SOUND: [DOORBELL]

AUNT ROSE: Oh, they're here. Come on! Come on!

SOUND: [DOOR OPEN]

AUNT ROSE: Oh, James, I'm so sorry. Well, hello there! You must be Mary. Oh, James, she looks just like her…

JAMES: [interrupting clearing throat] Mary, you remember your Aunt Rose?

AUNT ROSE: Oh, of course she doesn't remember, James. She was just a baby the last time I saw her. Well, what's wrong, dear? Not going to say hello?

JAMES: She's okay…just tired from the long flight.

AUNT ROSE: Oh, Ivan. This is Ivan. He worked for the family that owned the house before I bought it. He's sort of a caretaker and helps out around the house.

JAMES: Nice to meet you, Ivan.

IVAN: Yes, and you.

AUNT ROSE: Ivan, would you please take their bags upstairs to their rooms?

JAMES: Oh, that's not necessary. We can manage.

AUNT ROSE: Nonsense. Come inside. I want to show you and Mary around the house.

SOUND: [DOOR CLOSE]

AUNT ROSE: It will be so nice having you both here. You must think I'm crazy for buying such a large house just for myself. But, at the price I paid, it really was a bargain. Half what it's worth.

JAMES: It is a beautiful old house.

AUNT ROSE: The previous owners were anxious to sell it. Can you believe it? They were convinced it's haunted. [laughing] But, I don't believe in such nonsense.

MARY: Haunted?

AUNT ROSE: Oh, my dear, [laughing] there's nothing to worry about. Just a lot of silly superstition and nonsense.

IVAN: Bags are in the rooms.

AUNT ROSE: Thank you, Ivan. Come along, Mary, there's lots more to see—and I have a surprise for you.

JAMES: [irritated] Mary! Did you not hear your aunt? Why can't you do what you're told the first time?

AUNT ROSE: James! She's just tired. Come on, Mary, and let me show you what I have for you. I was looking through the attic the other day and found this.

SOUND: [DOLL SAYING: "Ma ma."]

MARY: A doll? Is that for me?

AUNT ROSE: Sure it is. You don't think you're too old to play with dolls do you?

MARY: I...I guess not.

JAMES: [irritated] Mary—what do you say?

MARY: Thank you.

AUNT ROSE: You're welcome, dear. The people I bought the house from left all sorts of things up in the attic. Looks like it might have been some kind of children's playroom a long time ago.

IVAN: The attic? The attic is not safe.

AUNT ROSE: Oh nonsense, Ivan. It's just dusty and needs a good cleaning.

IVAN: The attic is not safe. You should not go up there.

AUNT ROSE: Now, that's just silly. The only thing wrong with the attic is that there's no heat. The gas doesn't work up there. But, we will have that fixed soon enough. Come on, Mary. Help yourself to some lemonade. Ivan made it just this morning. James, come with me to the kitchen. I made fresh coffee right before you got here.

JAMES: After that long flight, coffee sounds great.

SOUND: [COFFEE POURING]

AUNT ROSE: Do you still take your coffee black?

JAMES: Yes, thank you.

SOUND: [GLASS BREAKING]

JAMES: MARY!

AUNT ROSE: Oh, she's dropped her lemonade. Watch out dear, those pieces of glass will cut you.

JAMES: [angry] You did that on purpose didn't you!

MARY: [pleading] No, daddy, I didn't mean to.

AUNT ROSE: James!

JAMES: [angry] I know you did! You did it on purpose!

AUNT ROSE: James, stop it! She didn't mean…

JAMES: [interrupting] Yes, she did! I know her.

AUNT ROSE: But why would she do it on purpose?

JAMES: Because she hates me! She wishes that I was killed in the accident instead of her mother!

AUNT ROSE: James! How could you say such a thing in front of that poor child? Hasn't she been through enough?

MARY: [sobbing] I'm sorry, Daddy.

AUNT ROSE: Mary, come here. It's okay; I know you didn't mean to do it. He didn't mean it. We've got to be patient with him.

MARY: [sobbing] Daddy doesn't love me anymore.

AUNT ROSE: Oh, sweetheart, your daddy loves you and he loved your mommy very much, too. He's just hurting right now, and when people hurt, it's harder for them to show their love. It's just going to take some time, but you'll feel his love again.

MARY: [sobbing] No, I won't. He didn't love me before. He won't ever.

AUNT ROSE: Oh, Mary, you're just upset. Your daddy loves you very much. Come on upstairs. I'll show you your room.

[MUSIC SCENE TRANSITION]

NARRATOR: The next day, Aunt Rose asked Ivan to help her gather cleaning supplies for the attic.

IVAN: The attic is not safe. We should not go up there.

AUNT ROSE: Yes, you keep saying that, Ivan, but that's nonsense. When it's clean and the gas is repaired, it will make the perfect playroom for Mary.

IVAN: No. The child should not play up there.

AUNT ROSE: That's just ridic… [interrupted by sounds of children talking] …ulous. What's that sound?

MARY: [from a distance] I don't understand.

ALICE: [from a distance] Yes, a long time ago.

SOUND: [DOOR OPENING]

AUNT ROSE: Mary! What are you doing in here? It's too cold to be in here. We have to clean up all this dust before you can play in here.

MARY: Yes, ma'am.

AUNT ROSE: Who were you talking to?

MARY: No one. Just Alice.

AUNT ROSE: Alice? Who's Alice?

MARY: Well, my doll of course! [laughing] Who else?

SOUND: [DOLL SAYING: "Ma ma."]

AUNT ROSE: All right, dear. [laughing] But until we get the gas repaired and have heat up here—AND get this mess cleaned up—you need to play in your room.

MARY: [disappointed] Yes, ma'am.

AUNT ROSE: Now run along, so we can get started cleaning.

MARY: Okay.

SOUND: [DOOR CLOSING]

IVAN: The attic is no place for the child.

AUNT ROSE: Ivan, you're starting to sound like a broken record. Help me get this mess cleaned up.

[MUSIC SCENE TRANSITION]

AUNT ROSE: Well, good morning!

MARY: Good morning. Can you help me with something?

AUNT ROSE: Sure, sweetheart, but don't you want some breakfast?

MARY: Not right now. Maybe later. Come on. [rapid footsteps followed by yelling from a distance] It's in here!

AUNT ROSE: All right. I'm coming. What is it, Mary?

MARY: Can you help me get the music box?

AUNT ROSE: Music box? What music box? There's only old boxes and luggage in that closet.

MARY: No, it's in there. Top shelf. Way in the back behind everything.

AUNT ROSE: What's your music box doing in there? You really should keep your things in your room.

MARY: It's not mine, but she said that I could have it.

AUNT ROSE: She? She who?

MARY: Alice.

AUNT ROSE: Oh? And who's Alice?

MARY: I told you. My doll!

SOUND: [BOXES HITTING FLOOR]

AUNT ROSE: I don't see any music box up here.

MARY: It's there. All the way in the back.

AUNT ROSE: Well, how in the world did that get up here. I've never seen this before.

SOUND: [MUSIC BOX]

MARY: She wants me to take it up to the attic.

AUNT ROSE: Who wants you to?

MARY: [pleading] I just told you…Alice.

AUNT ROSE: [sarcastically] Oh, right. Alice…your doll. [laughing] Well, okay. We have the attic all cleaned up, so you can use it as a playroom. But, put on a jacket until we have the heat working in there. Have fun dear!

MARY: [laughing and from a distance] Okay! We will!

[MUSIC SCENE TRANSITION]

JAMES: You're going to spoil that girl.

AUNT ROSE: Don't be silly. I spent one Saturday cleaning up the attic so she can have a playroom and now I'm having a gas pipe fixed. It was no trouble.

JAMES: She'll be tired of it in a week.

AUNT ROSE: Well, you could at least show some interest in what she's doing. That's probably why she's been sneaking up there without telling anyone. Talking to that doll all the time. She's just rebelling because she thinks you don't want her to have a playroom.

GAS MAN: Excuse me ma'am.

AUNT ROSE: Oh, yes, did you find out why the gas doesn't work up there? Was the pipe blocked?

GAS MAN: Well you know—I've been up in that attic all day trying to find the problem. There was no blockage. I put in all new pipe and it still doesn't work. Gas runs to every heater in the entire house. Just not up to the attic. It's the craziest thing I've ever seen. No explaining it.

AUNT ROSE: Well, we must have heat up there. What can we do?

GAS MAN: Ma'am, I've done all I can do. You'd better get yourself an electric heater, or something.

AUNT ROSE: Well, thanks, anyway.

JAMES: Great. Just great. Now I get to throw money away on an electric heater that she'll only use once or twice.

AUNT ROSE: James, you've really become a selfish person. Do you really want her to hate you? Will that make you feel better? Have her REALLY hate you, so you can feel even more sorry for yourself?

JAMES: Don't start in on me again.

AUNT ROSE: I'll tell you one thing. I don't have any pity for you. That girl loves you. At least you know…

MARY: [interrupting] Hi, Daddy…Aunt Rose.

AUNT ROSE: Hello, dear. I didn't hear you come down stairs.

MARY: Did the gas man leave?

AUNT ROSE: Yes. Unfortunately, he couldn't get the heater working up there.

MARY: Oh, I knew you wouldn't be able to.

AUNT ROSE: How did you know that?

MARY: Alice told me.

JAMES: Alice? Who's Alice?

MARY: This is Alice Daddy. Right here!

SOUND: [DOLL: "Ma ma."]

JAMES: That doll? [laughing] So, your doll talks to you?

MARY: Oh, yes, Daddy. She tells me all sorts of things.

JAMES: Now, Mary, pretending is one thing, but making up these stories about your doll talking to you…

MARY: [pleading] But I'm not making up anything, Daddy. It's true! Alice does talk to me. Tell him Aunt Rose. Tell him about the music box.

JAMES: Now listen here, young lady. If you don't stop this lying I'm taking that doll away from you!

SOUND: [FOOTSTEPS RUNNING AWAY]

MARY: No, Daddy, no! Not Alice! [yelling from a distance] I won't give her up. I just won't!

JAMES: Rose, this doll business has got to stop right now. She's too old for such foolishness.

AUNT ROSE: Maybe this doll has become real to her, but whose fault is that? You hardly even talk to her anymore. And who else does she have to talk to? A servant and an aunt she doesn't even know. Let me go see what I can do.

IVAN: Be careful. Do not interfere with Alice.

AUNT ROSE: [laughing] Her doll? Now that's funny. I'll be right back.

SOUND: [FOOTSTEPS]

MARY: [from a distance] But I don't think they believe me.

ALICE: [from a distance] I told you not to tell.

AUNT ROSE: Mary?

SOUND: [DOOR OPENING]

AUNT ROSE: [worried/a bit frightened] Mary, sit down. I think we need to talk.

SOUND: [DOLL DROPPING ON THE FLOOR, THEN SAYING: "Ma ma."]

[MUSIC SCENE TRANSITION]

JAMES: If I had my way, that doll would have ended up in the trash weeks ago.

IVAN: Alice is no doll.

JAMES: [sarcastically] Yeah, right!

IVAN: The doll only helps the child hide the truth.

JAMES: Truth? What truth?

IVAN: The attic is occupied by something else. The previous owners moved because of this.

JAMES: What are you trying to say, Ivan? The attic is haunted? [laughing]

IVAN: Yes, very haunted…but in the most friendliest of ways. Many years ago, a father of a little girl lived here. He left her alone in the house many nights. One night she was alone in the playroom…

SOUND: [WOMAN SCREAMING]

JAMES: [shouting] Rose! What's going on?

SOUND: [FOOTSTEPS RUNNING]

JAMES: What's going on in here?

AUNT ROSE: [frantic] James, get her out of here. Get her out of this attic. Something's in here! Something touched me! Then it tried to grab me!

MARY: She didn't mean to scare you, Aunt Rose. Alice says she's sorry.

ALICE: [whispering] I'm sorry.

AUNT ROSE: [frantic] James, we can't stay in this house. We've got to get out of here. Alice is not a doll! Not a doll at all!

JAMES: Would someone tell me what is going on?

IVAN: The child told me the story. Same story I have heard many times before. A girl died up here in the attic years ago from escaping gas.

JAMES: She could have heard that story from one of the neighbors.

IVAN: She has seen no neighbors. She has not left the house.

MARY: [pleading] No, Daddy; it was Alice. Alice told me!

AUNT ROSE: But, James, what about the music box? How did she know about the music box?

[MUSIC SCENE TRANSITION]

NARRATOR: How DID she know about the music box? A ghost story? The overactive imagination of a young girl? What about Rose? She said something grabbed her. More imagination? We like to think of it as another one of our…TALES FROM BEYOND.

UNBREAKABLE

CAST OF CHARACTERS (in order of appearance)

Narrator: Daniel Roebuck
Kate: Mary Elizabeth McGlynn
Bill: Robert Picardo
Receptionist: Betsy Rue
Frank: Kyle Hebert

Mary Elizabeth McGlynn thinks about her character and line delivery before recording "Unbreakable."

[MUSIC IN AND UNDER]

NARRATOR: That mysterious human connection. We've all heard of people who claim to be so closely connected to one another. So closely connected that they finish each other's sentences and can sense what the other is feeling, thinking, or experiencing. In our next tale, called "Unbreakable," we meet Bill and Kate. From the moment they met, they've shared this unbreakable connection. Without a word being spoken, they know each other's thoughts and emotions. They share a love that can weather any storm. But, that doesn't mean things didn't occasionally get a little…stormy.

SOUND: [thunder]

KATE: All you had to do is be nice.

BILL: Seems to me YOU were being nice enough for everyone!

KATE: And what is THAT supposed to mean?

BILL: You know exactly what I mean. Dancing with him. Drinking like there's no tomorrow. Hanging all over him all night like a cheap…

KATE: WHAT? You're the one who told me to be nice to him!

BILL: Sure! Polite conversation is nice! What you were doing was…

KATE: Was what? Embarrassing?

BILL: Yeah, actually…I was embarrassed. Embarrassed for myself and embarrassed for you the way you were carrying on.

KATE: Well, at least I made sure he was laughing and had a good time. You didn't say more than two words to him.

BILL: Maybe that's because I wanted to punch him in the FACE, the way he kept pouring drinks down you all night.

KATE: Wait a minute. You wait just a minute. It was your idea to give up your nice executive position where you and Frank could start your own advertising agency. It was your idea to go to this party and try to get his business. And it was YOU who told me to be nice to him. "Help me get this account," you said!

BILL: Yes, but all I wanted you to do was be nice. Polite. You didn't have to be so…

SOUND: [drink being poured]

BILL: Do you REALLY think you need another drink? Don't you think you've had enough?

KATE: OH! Here we go. You always know what's best for me. You always know what I need. What I don't need. Well, you're right. I've had enough! I've REALLY had enough!

SOUND: [FOOTSTEPS, DOOR OPEN, DOOR SLAMS SHUT]

BILL: Kate! Wait! Where are you going? Come back here! We're not done with this!

SOUND: [THUNDER]

SOUND: [DOOR OPENS, RAIN/THUNDER, CAR DOOR SHUTS, CAR STARTS UP, SPEEDS OFF]

BILL: [yelling—off microphone] Fine! Run away! At least you're good at that!

SOUND: [DOOR CLOSES]

BILL: [to himself] At least you're good at something. [heavy sigh]

SOUND: [THUNDER, RAIN]

SOUND: [FADE IN CAR ENGINE/SPEEDING CAR, RAIN/THUNDER, SCREECHING TIRES GOING AROUND CURVES]

KATE: [to herself and furious] I just can't stand him sometimes. Constantly complaining. Nothing's ever good enough for that man.

SOUND: [cell phone/text message]

KATE: Great. Just great. Where's that stupid phone?

NARRATOR: Looking for her cell phone and not paying attention to the road, Kate doesn't see the road construction signs ahead.

KATE: What the…

SOUND: [SCREECHING TIRES]

KATE: [screaming]

NARRATOR: Kate hits the brakes, but the slippery, wet road sends her car off of the side and down to the bottom of a ravine.

SOUND: [SCREECHING TIRES, CAR CRASH, RAIN/THUNDER/STORM SOUNDS]

[MUSIC SCENE TRANSITION]

SOUND: [alarm clock]

BILL: [yawn] Kate…wake up. Come on, it's time to get up. [yelling] Kate? Where are you? [to himself] Perfect. Just perfect. Stayed out all night, I guess. [yawning the following] Oh, I need coffee.

SOUND: [CELL PHONE—DIALING NUMBER]

BILL: [to himself] Come on. Answer the phone.

KATE: [voicemail message] Hi, this is Kate. I can't get to the telephone so leave your name and number and I will call you back.

BILL: [angry] Kate, it's 7 a.m.! Where are you?! Call me back!

SOUND: [CELL PHONE—CALL END BEEP]

BILL: Well, that's just GREAT. [heavy sigh] Coffee… I need coffee.

NARRATOR: Meanwhile, back at the crash site, the sound of Kate's cell phone ringing wakes her up.

SOUND: [CELL PHONE RINGING]

KATE: [weak, groggy and to herself] Ohhhhhh…my head. Where am I? What? What happened?

SOUND: [RE-PLAY CAR CRASH SOUNDS WITH KATE SCREAMING OVER NARRATION]

NARRATOR: Remembering she ran off the road last night, Kate awakens to find herself trapped in the wreckage of her own car.

KATE: Oh no! No, no, no, no, no…this can't be happening.

SOUND: [CELL PHONE STILL RINGING]

KATE: [weak but desperate] My phone. Where's my phone? Oh, I can't reach it. [weak/trying to yell, her voice drawn out] Bill…….

[MUSIC SCENE TRANSITION]

SOUND: [COFFEE POURING INTO CUP]

BILL: [breathing in smelling the coffee] Mmmmmm…coffee.

KATE: [weak and distant] Bill….

BILL: Well, it's about time you got home. I'm in the kitchen. Come get some coffee. Hurry up, you'll be late for work. Kate?

NARRATOR: Bill goes into the living room, but Kate is nowhere to be found. He searches the entire house, but no Kate.

BILL: [to himself] Huh! I could've swore I heard…Nah, she's probably at work already.

SOUND: [CELL PHONE—DIALING NUMBER]

RECEPTIONIST: Good morning. Thank you for calling…

BILL: [interrupting] Hello? It's Bill. Has Kate made it in to work yet?

RECEPTIONIST: No, we haven't seen her this morning. Is something wrong?

BILL: No, nothing's wrong. Just ask her to give me a call when she gets in, okay?

RECEPTIONIST: I'll give her the message. Are you sure everything's okay?

BILL: Yes, everything's fine. Just ask her to call me. Thanks.

SOUND: [CELL PHONE—CALL END BEEP]

BILL: [to himself] Well, I can't sit around here all day. Got to get to work. Maybe just one more cup of coffee first.

SOUND: [COFFEE POURING INTO CUP]

[MUSIC SCENE TRANSITION]

SOUND: [DOOR OPENING/CLOSING]

FRANK: Morning, Bill! How'd the party go last night?

BILL: [irritated] Fine. Everything's fine.

FRANK: Whoa, wait a minute, Bill. You don't sound so sure. Did we get his business or not?

BILL: No, everything went just great. I'm sure we'll get his business. [sarcastically] KATE made sure of that!

FRANK: Uh oh. What happened?

BILL: Just Kate being Kate. Drinking too much and making a fool of herself.

SOUND: [TELEPHONE RINGING AT A DISTANCE]

FRANK: That's my phone. Be right back.

BILL: [to himself] Yep. [heavy sigh] Just Kate being Kate.

FRANK: [yelling from a distance and getting closer] Bill! Hey Bill! Guess what?

BILL: [irritated] WHAT?

FRANK: [excited] We got the account! That was him on the phone. You're right. Everything must've went great last night because he's giving us ALL his advertising business!

BILL: [not so excited] Great. That's great.

FRANK: Whoa…Bill…this is GREAT news! What's wrong?

BILL: It's just…Kate. We had a huge fight when we got home last night and…

FRANK: Yeah, and?

BILL: Well…she never came home last night. I called her cell phone and left a message. I called her office and told them to have her call when she got in. I haven't heard anything from her. I've got this feeling I just can't shake. Like something's wrong. Terribly wrong!

SOUND: [ROAD CONSTRUCTION, HEAVY MACHINERY]

FRANK: Don't worry. I bet she's…

BILL: [interrupting] What's all that noise?

FRANK: What noise?

BILL: Outside—it sounds like they're working on the street.

KATE: [weak and distant] Bill….

BILL: Kate? Is that you?

SOUND: [ROAD CONSTRUCTION SOUNDS FADE]

FRANK: Are you okay? I don't hear anything!

BILL: [irritated] Well, it's gone now. Didn't you hear the noises outside? Didn't you hear Kate just calling my name?

FRANK: Maybe you need to go back home and get some rest! Kate's not here and there's nothing going on outside! Try giving Kate a call at work. I bet she's there and just didn't get the message.

BILL: You're probably right.

SOUND: [CELL PHONE—DIALING NUMBER]

RECEPTIONIST: Good morning. Thank you for call…

BILL: [interrupting] Hey, it's Bill again.

RECEPTIONIST: Hi—we still haven't seen her this morning.

BILL: Huh, still not in yet?

RECEPTIONIST: Do you think something's happened to her?

BILL: No, I'm sure everything's fine.

RECEPTIONIST: When you hear from her, please have her call us.

BILL: Yes, I'll have her call in as soon as I hear from her.

RECEPTIONIST: Have a good day!

BILL: Yes, you too. Thanks.

SOUND: [CELL PHONE—CALL END BEEP]

FRANK: I bet she's back at home sleeping it off. Come on. I'll drive you home. You need to take the day off and get some rest.

[MUSIC SCENE TRANSITION]

SOUND: [CAR PULLING UP, STOPPING/ENGINE OFF/ DOORS OPEN AND CLOSE]

BILL: See, she's not home. Her car would be parked right here in the driveway!

SOUND: [ROAD CONSTRUCTION, HEAVY MACHINERY]

BILL: There it is again! Construction noises…where's that coming from?

FRANK: What noises? I don't hear a thing! I'd better get you inside.

SOUND: [CONSTRUCTION NOISE FADES. KEYS OPENING DOOR]

KATE: [weak/at a distance] Bill…help me…

BILL: [worried] You had to have heard that. [calling out desperately] Kate?

FRANK: I didn't hear anything, Bill. Come on. Let's get you inside.

BILL: No, I heard Kate calling out to me. She's inside! Come on!

NARRATOR: Bill and Frank searched the entire house, but Kate was nowhere to be found. Bill just couldn't shake the feeling that Kate was in trouble and needed his help.

BILL: [yelling desperately] Kate!

FRANK: Just calm down. I'm sure she's fine. You need to lie down and rest.

BILL: No, something's wrong! I just know it! [yelling] Kate, where are you?

FRANK: Bill, she's not here. We've checked the house. It's almost noon. She must be at work by now.

BILL: [pleading] No, she's hurt! She needs my help! You've got to help me find her!

SOUND: [ROAD CONSTRUCTION, HEAVY MACHINERY]

BILL: There it is again. The construction noise. Can't you hear it!?

FRANK: There is no construction noise. Bill, the only road construction anywhere near here is miles away. Out on Highway 18.

KATE: [weak/at a distance] Bill…help me. Help me, Bill.

BILL: There she is again! [yelling] Kate! Kate, where are you?

SOUND: [CONSTRUCTION NOISE FADES]

FRANK: Okay, I think I need to take you to the doctor. You're delirious.

BILL: No, I'm not! It's Kate! She's in trouble. She's out there and needs our help!

FRANK: She's out there? Out where? What are you talking about?

BILL: [almost hysterical] The road construction! Out on highway 18! That's where she is. She's hurt and needs our help! Frank! Please…HELP ME.

FRANK: Okay, okay. Calm down. I'll drive you out there. Just calm down.

[MUSIC SCENE TRANSITION]

SOUND: [CAR DRIVING SOUNDS]

FRANK: Why don't you call her office again?

BILL: No, she's not at work. I just know she's out here somewhere.

FRANK: Okay, relax. We're almost to the road construction site.

BILL: [muttering] Just hold on, Kate. I'm coming. Almost there.

FRANK: What?

BILL: [irritated] Faster! Can't you drive any faster?!

FRANK: Look, up ahead. There's the road construction.

BILL: Frank, stop the car! Stop right here!

SOUND:	[CAR COMING TO STOP/ENGINE OFF/ DOORS OPEN]
SOUND:	[CONSTRUCTION SOUNDS AT A DISTANCE]
FRANK:	See Bill, she's not here. She's nowhere in sight.
BILL:	Look! Up ahead! See it? On the road! Come on!
SOUND:	[FOOTSTEPS RUNNING ON PAVEMENT]
BILL:	See the tire skid marks on the road?
FRANK:	Looks like they go off the side here.
BILL:	I'm calling her cell phone.
SOUND:	[CELL PHONE—DIALING NUMBER]
SOUND:	[CELL PHONE RINGING AT A DISTANCE]
BILL:	Listen, do you hear that?! It's Kate's phone!
FRANK:	Look down there! Through those trees at the bottom of the ravine…Is that a car?
BILL:	[yelling down] Kate!
KATE:	[from a distance/weak] Bill, help me.
FRANK:	I don't believe it. I just don't believe it!

BILL: I'm going down there. Frank, call 911. [yelling down] Kate! Hold on! I'm coming!

FRANK: I just don't believe it. You knew she was here. But how did you know?

[MUSIC SCENE TRANSITION]

NARRATOR: How did he know? How COULD he know? Another incredible coincidence? Some mysterious form of human communication? Telepathy, perhaps? We like to call it another one of our…TALES FROM BEYOND.

Photo Gallery

We now invite you to take a glimpse inside the studio to experience a few behind-the-scenes moments in the making of *TALES FROM BEYOND*.

Co-director/Co-writer Jim O'Rear outside the Los Angeles studio where *Tales From Beyond* was recorded.

DANIEL ROEBUCK | Daniel Roebuck has enjoyed working in a number of horror movies—his favorite genre. He has collaborated with filmmaker Rob Zombie on *Halloween, Halloween 2, Devil's Rejects,* and *Lords of Salem.* He also appeared in Don Coscarelli's cult favorite *Bubba Ho Tep,* as well as the director's *Reggie's Tales* and *John Dies At The End.*

Daniel has played countless characters on sometimes "creepy" shows. Some of his most memorable have been in *Grimm, Star Trek, Next Generation,* and *Ghost Whisperer.* Behind the camera, Roebuck has produced, written, and directed/co-directed a number of documentaries including *Halloween: The Happy Haunting of America* and its sequel, as well as *Goolians, Movieland Memories* ,and a number of documentaries for the *Monsterama* series.

Daniel Roebuck and Jim O'Rear like to lighten the atmosphere of the studio.

Co-director/Co-writer Keven Herren directs Robert Picardo on subtle character traits regarding his character in "Unbreakable."

Mary Elizabeth McGlynn (*Blade, Iron Man, Bleach, Naruto, X-Men, The Avengers*).

Jim O'Rear clowns around with Betsy Rue and Mary Elizabeth McGlynn, showing that they can never be too serious in the studio.

e Hebert (*Dragonball Z, Wreck It ph, Naruto, Blade, The Avengers*).

KYLE HEBERT | In high school and at the University of North Texas, Kyle Hebert was a DJ for the schools' radio stations. Not long after graduation, he worked his way through many radio formats and eventually found a home on Disney Radio.

Over the last decade he pursued his other great interest: voice acting. At Funimation, he voiced many characters, including teenage Gohan of *Dragonball-Z* fame. This has propelled him into celebrity status in the Anime world, with world appearances and websites devoted to his work. Other notable roles include: Soul Eater (*Masamune*), Ouran High School Host Club (*Kazukiyo Soga*), Fullmetal Alchemist (*Vato Falman*), Tales of Symphonia (*Richter Abend*) and Star Ocean (*Dias, Arumat, Crow*). Kyle also provides voices in numerous video games, including *Final Fantasy XIII, World of Warcraft, Devil May Cry 4, Dynasty Warriors,* and James Cameron's *Avatar*.

Betsy Rue (*True Blood, My Bloody Valentine 3D, Halloween 2, The Mentalist*).

Jim O'Rear discusses recording options and microphone placement with his studio engineer.

Daniel Roebuck listens to direction about the portrayal of his character from Co-director/Co-writer Jim O'Rear.

BETSY RUE | Betsy Rue is an American actress and pop singer, best known for her roles in My Bloody Valentine 3D and Halloween II. She has also appeared in many TV series, including Unfabulous, How I Met Your Mother, According to Jim, True Blood, Eastwick, and iCarly.

Betsy Rue takes a moment to study some lines before recording "Deadly Fortune."

Kyle Hebert watches as Mary Elizabeth McGlynn and Daniel Roebuck prepare characterizations.

Co-director/Co-writer Kevin Herren does some last-minute recording equipment placement as Robert Picardo studies his lines.

ROBERT PICARDO was born on October 27, 1953, in Philadelphia, Pennsylvania, where he spent his whole childhood. He graduated from the William Penn Charter School and attended Yale University. At Yale, he landed a role in Leonard Bernstein's *Mass* and, at age 19, he played a leading role in the European premiere of *Mass*. Later, he graduated with a Bachelor's degree in Drama from Yale University. He appeared in the David Mamet play *Sexual Perversity in Chicago* and wth Diane Keaton in *The Primary English Class*. In 1977, he made his Broadway debut in the comedy hit *Gemini* with Danny Aiello, and also appeared in Bernard Slade's *Tribute, Beyond Therapy*, as well as *Geniuses* and *The Normal Heart*, for which he won a Drama-Logue Award.

Then, he became involved in television, where he soon was nominated for an Emmy Award for his role as Coach Cutlip on the series *The Wonder Years* (1988). Robert appeared in several other series: *China Beach* (1988), *Frasier* (1993), *Ally McBeal* (1997), *Home Improvement* (1991), *The Outer Limits* (1995) and *Sabrina, the Teenage Witch* (1996). In 1995, he got the role of the holographic doctor on *Star Trek: Voyager* (1995), where he also directed two episodes. Other roles include *The Howling* (1981), *Star 80* (1983), *Get Crazy* (1983), *Oh, God! You Devil* (1984), *Innerspace* (1987), *Munchies* (1987), *Samantha* (1992), *White Mile* (1994), *Star Trek: First Contact* (1996), *Small Soldiers* (1998), *Looney Tunes: Back in Action* (2003), *Quantum Quest: A Cassini Space Odyssey* (2010), and more.

He resides in Los Angeles, California, with his wife, Linda, and their two daughters.

Robert Picardo prepares to step up to the microphone. (*Star Trek: Voyager, Stargate: SG-1, China Beach, Batman, Legend*).

Jim O'Rear did his best to distract Robert Picardo while he was working. It didn't work.

Daniel Roebuck takes a moment to feel out the characterization of his next reading.

Daniel Roebuck and Betsy Rue discuss having their scripts available in their smart phones.

Daniel Roebuck and Kyle Hebert get their script in place for the easiest and quietest page turning to be applied.

Mary Elizabeth McGlynn prepares to fire up the iPad, where she has her script stored.

MARY ELIZABETH MCGLYNN | Mary Elizabeth McGlynn is an American voice actress, ADR director, writer, and singer, best known for her extensive English-language dubbing of anime and her singing in multiple games from the *Silent Hill* series, as well as the movie adaptation, and *Dance Dance Revolution EXTREME*. She has also had several movie roles. She is the winner of an American Anime Award for Best Female Voice Actress for her role as Major Motoko Kusanagi in *Ghost In The Shell: Stand Alone Complex*. You can hear her as "Sei" in *Alpha Protocol* and "Nora" in *Final Fantasy XIII*. Some of her other popular roles are "Cornelia" in *Code Geasm*, "Kurenai" from *Naruto*, "Julia" from *Cowboy Bebop*, "Helba" and "Bordeau" from *.hack*, "Jagura" from *Wolf's Rain*, and "Caroline" from *Vampire Hunter D*.

She is currently directing *Naruto: Shippuden* for Disney XD and has directed the 4 *Naruto* movies, as well as *Naruto* the series, for which she received the 2008 SPJA award for best director. Among her many other directing credits are: *Cowboy Bebop* the series, *Cowboy Bebop: Knockin' on Heaven's Door*, *Wolf's Rain*, and the movie *Appleseed*. She was a co-writer for the American adaptation of *Metropolis*. She also directed the original animated series *Gormiti Lords of Nature* for Cartoon Network and *Wild Animal Babies* for PBS. For the gaming world, she directed Samuel L. Jackson and Ron Perlman in the *Afro Samurai* game, and the entire cast of *iCarly* for their interactive game. Mary Elizabeth has directed the voice work for *Soul Calibur Legends, Resident Evil: Umbrella Chronicles, Devil May Cry 3, 3.5* and *4, Spyhunter*, the *Naruto Clash of Ninja* and *Ultimate Ninja* series, as well being second director for *Kung Fu Panda*.

Jim O'Rear and Mary Elizabeth McGlynn share a friendly moment on the couch during a break in recording.

Co-director/Co-writer Jim O'Rear gets serious for a moment to record the character of Carnival Barker in "Deadly Fortune."

Kyle Hebert warns Robert Picardo to stay out of "The Attic."

TALES FROM BEYOND

STARRING

DANIEL ROEBUCK

ROBERT PICARDO

BETSY RUE

JIM O'REAR

KYLE HEBERT

MARY ELIZABETH MCGLYNN